Blossom Flower

and the
Enchanted Garden

DELISA SMITH

Illustrated by Adrian Cuevas del Valle

Blossom Flower and the Enchanted Garden

ISBN: 978-0-578-85755-8 (Paperback)

Printed in the United States

PROJECT MANAGER: Kassandra White
INTERIOR LAYOUT AND JACKET DESIGN: Vince Embry Rivera

Dedication

This is dedicated to my grandson, Tyler Jacob Ford. Thank you for inspiring me to write again. Love you from here to infinity.

Delisa Smith

Contents

CHAPTER 1

The Garden

Trudy loved flowers, so she and her mother planted a garden in their backyard. Everyday, Trudy would visit the garden. She took very good care of her garden. She watered the plants, gave them fertilizer, removed all the weeds, and made sure they had lots of sunlight. Trudy would even read and talk to the flowers.

There were different kinds of flowers in the garden. Trudy had planted pansies, marigolds, red trumpet vines, daffodils, lillies, and roses. She gave each flower a name and planted them in groups. Her favorite was a Royal Sunset Lily. Unlike the other lillies, she was purple-pink and peach when she bloomed.

Trudy took great care of her flowers, but she didn't know that the love and care she gave her flowers made them very special. Even though Trudy could not hear them, she imagined they had an enchanted world and came to life in the garden.

Her imagination created a whole world of flowers living a happy life. Each flower group had parents and children. Together they formed a beautiful bouquet. Everyone knew one another in this enchanted world of make believe.

CHAPTER 2

Inside the Garden

One day the sunrise came early, and the sunrays lit up the garden. The head Red Trumpet Vine Flower, Corey, blew out his morning trumpet sound. "Wake up, wake up, the sun is here."

Blossom Flower stretched out her leaves and spread out her petals. "Good morning, Dad. Good morning, Mom," Blossom chimed. She looked at her brother Carl, and said, "Wake up, sleepy head. It's a new day." Her sister, Shelly, yawned and wiped her eyes.

"Good morning, Blossom," Shelly mumbled.

The budding young flowers hurried to the fountain in the yard. After the fountain rinsed them clean, the young flowers headed off to the Botanical Elementary School.

On their way to school, Carl nearly fell in a hole. "Watch Out!" cried Shelly.

Blossom said, "I wonder what this hole is for."

"It was not here before," replied Carl. The siblings walked around the hole, to get to school.

When Blossom, Carl, and Shelly got to school, everyone was talking about the hole in the ground. Other flowers had their own idea of how the hole got there. There were so many different stories, but no one knew for sure.

After school got out, the hole was still there. So, the flowers hurried home to see if their parents knew why the hole was there. "Hi Mom and Dad," said Blossom.

Blossom could not say another word before Shelly yelled, "What is that hole for?"

Mom and Dad sat the young flowers down around the table. Dad calmed the young flowers down and told them not to worry. "Good things come from the ground," he said. Each time there is a hole in the ground, we get new members to our families.

As the night went on, the flowers were thrilled. Maybe they may get a new member to their family. The young flowers did their homework, ate their dinner, and went to bed. The morning could not come fast enough.

CHAPTER 3

The New Flower

Every day the garden of flowers would check to see if the hole was filled. A few days went by, but it was still empty. One evening the flowers heard a loud rumbling, and then rain started to fall. It seemed as if it would be a long night.

The next morning the trumpet flower, Corey, sounded his morning greeting, but this time he yelled. "They're here. They're here!"

All the flowers ran to the place where the hole was. But to their surprise the hole was gone, and three buds stood in its place.

The buds were unusual to the others. They had long green stems, with lots of leaves. The bud was round shaped and closed with pointy ends. Even though they were different than others in the garden, everyone was excited to see how they would look once they bloomed. Who would get new members to their family?

There were whispers all day about the new buds. Blossom watched the clock on the wall, waiting for the end of the day. It was the last day before Spring break, and the time was moving slow. As soon as the bell rang, the school was empty. Everyone rushed to the buds. But to their surprise, they still had not bloomed.

The sun came up, but the trumpet flower did not sound. All the flowers came out to see what happened. The buds had bloomed!

All the parents greeted the new members to the garden. "Hello, Welcome!" they said. The children were quiet and in awe because the new flowers were not like any other groups in the garden. The bloomed flowers had a lot of bright yellow petals and round brown faces.

There was a Mom, Dad, and daughter. They looked around and all said at once, "Hello."

Blossom's younger sister, Shelly, peeked her head through the crowd. "What kind of flowers are you?" she asked.

"We're the Sunflowers," said the mother sunflower.

"I am Dave. This is my wife, Clair, and this is our daughter, Sandy Sunflower," explained the father.

After they all met, everyone returned home.

CHAPTER 4

Talking to Someone New

Some groups were sad they did not get new members to their families. Others were not pleased that the sunflowers were different. One of the pansies complained, "They are tall and block the sunlight." No one was friendly to the Sunflowers.

The Sunflowers did not fell very welcomed in the garden. So, they stayed to themselves. It was like no one knew how to talk anymore. Or, they just could not find the right words to say.

Soon, Spring break was over, and the sprouting buds headed back to school. When class begin, Mrs. Iris, a Black Iris flower, stood before the room. Her black petals were smooth and shimmered. She wore her glasses at the end of her nose, with pretty hazel eyes that peeked over the top.

"Welcome back!" Mrs. Iris said. "It's so good to see you." She walked over to the door and then cleared her throat before saying, "I am happy to say we have a new student." She turned the doorknob and pulled the door open. "Say hello to Sandy Sunflower," she told the class.

"Hello Sandy Sunflower," they shouted in unison.

Mrs. Iris sat Sandy right next to Blossom. They looked at each other and smiled.

Later when lunch came, Sandy sat alone. Blossom thought this was her chance, she wanted to know about Sandy. Blossom walked over to Sandy, and introduced herself, "Hello, I'm Blossom."

From just that one hello, they were able to open up and talk. They seemed to like some of the same things. After school they talked and talked.

Blossom found out more about Sandy. They talked so much; their parents had to call them in for dinner.

CHAPTER 5

True to a Friend

Before class the next day, Blossom and Sandy saw each other in the school yard. "Hey Blossom," yelled Sandy.

Everyone looked at Blossom to see how she would reply. Blossom smiled, waved her leaf, and said, "Hey Sandy!"

The pansies, marigolds, and daffodils were not happy that Blossom and Sandy were friends. "I can't believe she is talking to her," said Susie Pansy.

"She will not sit with us for lunch," said Mary Marigold.

33

So, when Blossom walked toward them, they tooted up
their noses and turned away from her.

Blossom was hurt by her friends' actions. Then she saw Sandy, and they went to eat lunch together. Oh, how they laughed and giggled. They laughed and giggled so much that the pansies, marigolds, and daffodils couldn't stop staring.

Darla Daffodil walked over to Blossom and Sandy. "What's so funny?" Darla asked. "Stop laughing," she continued.

Soon Susie and Mary walked over as well. "You are our friend," Susie pouted.

"You don't laugh like that with us," huffed Mary.

Blossom looked up at her three friends' frowning faces. She smiled and said, "Sandy, these are my three friends Susie Pansy, Mary Marigold, and Darla Daffodil."

Sandy's face lit up. "Hey girls!" she said.

"Do you want to sit down and join us?" asked Blossom.

Blossom began telling the others all the new things she found out about Sandy. "Do you know sunflowers come from North America? There are also lilies there, too."

"Wow!" said Susie Pansy.

After a short time, all the girls were talking and laughing like old friends.

Blossom ran home to tell her mother about her day. She told her what she learned. She started by saying, "Hello helps you meet new people." Then she told her mother an important lesson she learned, "When someone is different, treat them kind."

"Also, talk and ask questions to understand more about them. You may find you have things in common," replied Blossom's Mom.

"I've learned so much today," said Blossom. "But, the most important thing was, you don't have to choose friends. You can be friends with everyone."

THE END

Made in the USA
Las Vegas, NV
16 April 2021